Francis William Bourdillon

The Night has a Thousand Eyes

And other Poems

Francis William Bourdillon

The Night has a Thousand Eyes
And other Poems

ISBN/EAN: 9783744764704

Printed in Europe, USA, Canada, Australia, Japan

Cover: Foto ©Andreas Hilbeck / pixelio.de

More available books at **www.hansebooks.com**

THE NIGHT HAS
A THOUSAND EYES

AND

OTHER POEMS

BY

F. W. BOURDILLON

BOSTON
LITTLE, BROWN, AND COMPANY
1899

University Press
John Wilson and Son, Cambridge, U.S.A.

THE ILLUSTRATIONS

BY

EDMUND H. GARRETT.

AILES D'ALOUETTE

When like a lark the soul upsprings,
Of verse she makes her airy wings.

Oh may these verses, pair and pair,
Some heart in heavenward flight upbear.

CONTENTS.

9

THE NIGHT HAS
A THOUSAND EYES.

THE night has a thousand eyes,
    And the day but one:
Yet the light of the bright world dies
    With the dying sun.

The mind has a thousand eyes,
    And the heart but one:
Yet the light of a whole
        life dies
    When love is done.

13

IN AN ALBUM.

As a faded flower
  Found in a book
Brings back some hour,
  Some word or look;

So, though ill-wrought
  My verses be,
May they bring one thought
  Of thy friend to thee!

·

A VALENTINE.

WHAT is my wish for thee, sweet Valentine?
　　A song of Spring, while Winter yet is here,
　　Heralding Summer in the silent year,
　　　　Be thine!

And for myself canst thou my wish divine?
　　To think my greeting may be in thy sight
　　Welcome as Summer's heralds, — this delight
　　　　Be mine!

IN APRIL.

WHAT tidings hath the swallow heard
    That bid her leave the lands of Summer
For woods and fields, where April yields
    Bleak welcome to the blithe new-comer?

O heart, that hast despaired of Spring,
    Learn the sweet lesson of the swallow.
To have no fear, though days be drear,
    But sunshine and soft airs must follow!

AN APRIL SHOWER.

THE primrose head is bowed with tears,
    The wood is rippling through with rain,
Though now the heaven once more appears,
    And beams the bounteous sun again.
From every blade and blossom-cup
The earth sends thankful incense up.

O happy hearts of flower and field,
    That soon as grief be overpast
Your fragrant thankfulness can yield
    For troubled skies and rainful blast!
I would that I as soon could see
The blessings of adversity!

A SPRING EVENING.

ACROSS the glory of the evening skies
   A veil is drawn of shadowed mists that rise
   From lavishness of God's late gift the rain.

So, after farewell said, fond memories
   Of words and looks the sweetest come again
   Across the glowing heart, a veil of pain.

JUNE IN LONDON.

SOUNDS of the riverside are in my ear
   Through the long day;
The merry haymakers I plainly hear,
   The tossing hay.

O cruel dreams, that through the roaring
         town
      Mine ears engage!
Alas, poor lark! whose home was once
         the down,
      But now a cage!

A BIRTHDAY IN NOVEMBER.

WHAT bird's song for her birthday can I find?
    What blossom by the rain not rent and bowed?
What green-left spray, of summer to remind,
    When woods are leafless, and the wind is loud?

Sweeter my song shall be than wood-birds sing,
    Fairer my flower than summer rose shall prove,
Greener my leaf-crown than the woods in spring,
    A simple verse that breathes of living love.

A DECEMBER GREETING.

FLOWERS I give for a gift of flowers,
    Lilies with lilies pay;
Yours were a gift of golden hours,
    But how can mine be gay?

My flowers are verses, the sad year's last,
    Yet haply not all in vain,
For the grace of your gift to my soul has passed, —
    May it here be given again!

DECAY.

O LUSTRE of decay!
    The daylight glides away
In glow of richer glory than at noon;
Autumn, that steals the flower,
Gives the tree golden dower,
And crimsons walls that will be leafless soon.

O dimness of decay!
The sunset hastes away,
And leaves the world the lone and darkling night;
And Autumn when he flies
Leaves only howling skies,
And trees that toss their naked boughs in fright.

LATET ANGUIS.

AH! full of purest influence
    On human mind and mood,
Of holiest joy to human sense
    Are river, field, and wood;
And better must all childhood be
That knows a garden and a tree.

For where can one diviner gleam
    On leagues of houses lie?
And what of Heaven can childhood dream
    That scarce has seen the sky?
Yet sin and sorrow's pedigree
Spring from a Garden and a Tree.

THE TROUBLED SEA.

THE weary ever-wandering waves,
     That know no change from their unrest,
Make murmuring in hollow caves,
     And sighing on the soft sand's breast,
That they forever to and fro
Beneath the pitiless sky must go.

The toiling tempest-driven ships,
     That buffet with the angry foam,
Escape at last its hungry lips
     And hail their white-cliffed harbor-home.
But the wild waves no rest may know,
But toss forever to and fro.

24

ONE DEED OF GOOD.

IF I might do one deed of good,
   One little deed before I die,
Or think one noble thought that should
   Hereafter not forgotten lie,
I would not murmur though I must
Be lost in Death's unnumbered dust.

The filmy wing, that wafts the seed
   Upon the careless wind to earth,
Lives only for a moment's deed,
   To find the germ fit place for birth;
For one swift moment of delight
It whirls, — then withers out of sight.

SURSUM CORDA.

HOW can the out-worn heart
　　To earth that clings
From self-spun cerements start
　　On rainbow wings?

How from its husk had flown
　　The butterfly
Save with its wings were grown
　　Love of the sky?

Y WYDDFA.

THE SUMMIT OF SNOWDON.

THE Place of Presence! Viewless phantoms crowd
    In mist and cloud;
And in dark chasm and deep abyss beneath
    Hides dreadful Death.

Not his nor theirs the Presence nor the Place!
    Close to the face
Of Heaven we stand, and more in love than fear
    Feel God is here.

SIGHT AND INSIGHT.

BY land and sea I travelled wide;
  My thought the earth could span;
And wearily I turned and cried
  "O little world of man!"

I wandered by a greenwood's side
  The distance of a rod;
My eyes were opened, and I cried
  "O mighty world of God!"

WITHIN THE GENTLE HEART LOVE SHELTERS HIM,
AS BIRDS WITHIN THE GREEN SHADE OF THE GROVE.

L OVE in the heart is as a nightingale
   That sings in a green wood;
And none can pass unheeding there, nor fail
   Of impulses of good.

Though cruel brief be Love's bright hour of song,
   Yet let him sing his fill!
For other hearts the echoes shall prolong
   When Love's own voice is still.

SAPPHIRES.

WONDERFUL is the sea,
    And the sky above the hill,
But the eyes of a maiden be
    More wondrous still.

For not the nightly skies
    Such depths discover,
As, when she loves, her eyes
    Do to her lover.

ADORATION.

MAIDEN, do you wonder why my eyes
    So deeply gaze in thine?
Not alone because night's clearest skies
    With no such lustre shine;

But that deep within the world there lies
    A mystery divine;
And I know not where, save in such eyes,
    To worship at its shrine.

CÆLI.

IF stars were really watching eyes
  Of angel armies in the skies,
I should forget all watchers there,
And only for your glances care.

And if your eyes were really stars
With leagues that none can mete for bars
To keep me from their longed-for day,
I could not feel more far away.

A REPROACH AND THE ANSWER.

THE Sun cried to the laughing Sea,
  " Leave thy sweet wiling!
Hast thou no depths of love in thee,
    Too deep for smiling?"
But ever, till the day was done,
The Sea turned laughing to the Sun.

But in the darkness and the storm,
    Could he discover
What terrors toss, what fears deform
    His laughing lover?
Oh, vainly love prays love look sad
When his mere presence makes her glad.

SEAWEED.

ALAS, poor weed! The careless tide
   Has left thee with his lightest foam;
And now a desert drear and wide
   Divides thee from thy wished-for home.
The tide may bear thee back once more,
But canst thou live thy life of yore?

Alas, I too am left awhile
   By her I love in lightest play;
On distant loves I see her smile,
   I hear her laughter far away.
Her heart may turn to me again,
But can my heart forget the pain?

O LOVE FORGIVE.

O LOVE forgive!
The sunny slopes forgive the passing cloud,
　　　And we who live
Less near to heaven than they should be less
　　proud.

　　　No punishment
Can pass the pain e'er to have grieved thee;
　　　And I present
My heart thus chastened thy new slave to be.

'TWIXT THEE AND ME.

I WILL not reason why I love,
    Or what I love in thee.
There breathes some secret from above
    In every flower we see.

Suddenly as we pass we own
    Some glimpse or scent divine.
Such secret to none others known
    My heart has found in thine.

I GIVE MY HEART.

I GIVE my heart! An empty hand
    Were never gift to thee!
But oh, that thou couldst understand
    What means this gift from me!

No mist that melts into the air,
    Nor rain into the sea,
Doth more its whole of being share
    Than I do, love, with thee!

IN A DISTANT LAND.

MY heart has wandered far from me
  On wings of love to-night,
Has passed a thousand leagues of sea
  Swifter than swallow's flight.

What doth thy journey profit thee,
  Thou idle wanderer,
Who canst not take my eyes to see
  Nor tongue to talk with her!

A SONG.

WHEN softer breezes blow
    And Winter flies,
How blue the rivers flow
    Beneath blue skies!

Ah, darling, it is sweet
    After long pain
When your glad eyes repeat
    My love again!

A WHITE DOVE ON A THUNDER-CLOUD.

A WHITE dove on a thunder-cloud,
    A white sail on a sullen sea;
But sail nor dove is white as love
    That in sorrow came to me.

The white dove fled, and tempest came :
    The white sail vanished from the sea;
But my white dove that is my true love
    Can never depart from me.

A MOMENT.

WHEN the lightning flashes by night,
    The raindrops seem
A million jewels of light
    In the moment's gleam.

And often in gathering fears
    A moment of love
To jewels will turn the tears
    That it cannot remove.

THE SHADOW OF LOVE.

THE branching shades in woodland glades
  Seem to the under fern
Wide as the night that leaves no light,—
  No shape can they discern.

And we who seek in senses weak
  Love's form to entertain —
So far Love's whole o'erspreads the soul —
  Too oft see only pain.

FAST AND LOOSE.

LOVE holds me so!
   I would that I could go!
I flutter up and down, and to and fro,
In vain; Love holds me so!

Love let me go.
I seek him high and low;
I wander up and down, and to and fro,
In vain, in vain; and life is cruel woe,
Since Love has let me go.

LOVE'S MEINIE.

THERE is no summer ere the swallows come,
    Nor Love appears.
  Till Hope, Love's light-winged herald, lifts
      the gloom
    Of years.

  There is no summer left when swallows fly,
    And Love at last,
  When hopes which filled its heaven droop
      and die,
  Is past.

A LOST VOICE.

A THOUSAND voices fill my ears
   All day until the light grows pale:
But silence falls when night-time nears,
   And where art thou, sweet nightingale?

Was that thine echo, faint and far?
   Nay, all is hushed as heaven above;
In earth no voice, in heaven no star,
   And in my heart no dream of love.

A GHOST.

I MET a ghost in an old bare house,
   That looked with lustreless eyes at me,
And drove from my eyes sweet dreams and drowse,
   Till the morning made it flee.

My house is builded of years decayed,
   And in vain I fill it with new glad light,
For a love that is lost is a ghost unlaid
   That troubles the silent night.

46

A LOST LOVE.

AS our childhood's world of wood and field,
  That strangers now possess;
As a dead mother's face in sleep revealed
  To her child in its loneliness;

As a dream of home to an exile banished
  Forever beyond the sea, —
So vainly sweet, O love long vanished,
  Is the sound of thy name to me!

GATHERED ROSES.

ONLY a bee made prisoner,
    Caught in a gathered rose!
Was he not 'ware a flower so fair
    For the first gatherer grows?

Only a heart made prisoner,
    Going out free no more!
Was he not 'ware a face so fair
    Must have been gathered before?

DROPPED PRIMROSES.

THEY grew in the grassy byway,
　　With the hazel wands o'erhead;
They lie in the dusty highway,
　　Dying or dead.

O flowers too soon forsaken!
　　O tender hearts grief-torn!
By a light love idly taken,
　　And left forlorn!

AFTER LOVE'S DEATH.

AFTER the sunshine, night;
    After the summer, rain;
After days of delight
    Come days of pain.

After the darkness, light;
    After the winter, spring.
After Love's death, delight,
    Ah, who can bring!

LIGHT AT EVENTIDE.

WHAT heart except to die can find
    The rain-beat, roses,
Though storms be past and heaven grow kind
    Ere daylight closes?

O sunless lives, long taught to bend
    By years of sadness,
What can ye do if sorrows end
    But die of gladness?

WAITING.

WHEN rose-leaves in long grasses fall
　　To hide their shattered head,
All tenderly the grasses tall
　　Bow down to veil the dead.

And there are hearts content to wait,
　　Still as the grasses lie,
Till those they love, however late,
　　Turn there at last to die.

THE DIFFERENCE.

SWEETER than voices in the scented hay,
  Or laughing children gleaning ears astray,
Or Christmas songs that shake the snows above,
Is the first cuckoo, when he comes with love.

Sadder than birds on sunless summer eves,
Or drip of raindrops on the autumn leaves,
Or wail of wintry waves on frozen shore,
Is spring that comes but brings us love no more.

DE PROFUNDIS.

BELOW the dark waves where the dead go down
    Are gulfs of night more deep;
But little care they whom the waves once drown
    How far from light they sleep.

But who, in deepest sorrow though he be,
    Fears not a deeper still?
Would God that sorrow were as the salt sea,
    Whose topmost waters kill!

RELIEF.

BLANK has the day been,
  Blind all the sky;
White has the way been,
  Chill the snows lie.

Only at nightfall,
  Heard faint and low,
Hark! 'tis the light fall,
  Rain on the snow.

DO THE DEAD THINK OF THE LIVING?

DO the dead think of the living,
  In the blue heaven overhead,
All repenting, all forgiving,
  As the living of the dead?

Yes: but while we weep, surveying
  Pathways long and lonely feet,
They in heaven smile softly, saying,
  "'Tis to-morrow and we meet!"

EARTH'S ANGELS.

WHAT though no more in human guise,
　　On radiant pinions borne,
Are angels seen of mortal eyes,—
　　Earth is not left forlorn.

Some bird that sings in hopeless hours
　　God's messenger may be;
And I have seen in primrose flowers
　　God's angels smile on me.

ANGELS' TEARS.

THE lily weeps at even,
    For vapors fallen anew
From the clear vault of heaven
    Turn at her touch to dew.
'Tis only so heaven's tearless eyes
With mortal woes can sympathize.

Know ye the white-souled maiden
    That's like the lily bell?
When her soft eyes are laden
    With teardrops, men may tell
The angels' sympathy appears,
Made visible in human tears.

i

PATIENCE.

STILL are the ships that at anchor ride,
  Waiting fair winds or turn of the tide;
Nothing they fret, though they go not yet
Out on the glorious ocean wide.
O wild hearts, that yearn to be free,
Look and learn from the ships of the sea!

Bravely the ships in the tempest tossed
Buffet the waves till the sea be crossed;
Not in despair of the haven fair,
Though winds blow backward, and leagues be lost.
O weary hearts that yearn for sleep,
Look and learn from the ships on the deep!

SO LONG AGO.

CHILD of the dark eyes, do you know
   What it is makes me kiss you so?
     'Tis that your eyes are dark and deep,
     And love in their low depths seems to sleep,
As in those of my love when he kissed me so,
     Long ago, ah! long ago.

Child of the dark hair, can you guess
Why from your head I cut a tress?
     Because his lock, of the same dark hue,
     I burnt in scorn when he proved untrue.
But now I could look on it calmly, so,
     It was so long, so long ago.

A LA CHALEUR DU JOUR.

LANDS of our childish dreams,
　　Of flowers and happy streams,
　Too far, too far beyond recall ye fade.
　Children and butterflies,
　What gain ye, growing wise,
　To make amends for happiness decayed?

　The wood's enchanted ways,
　Trees that were haunts of fays,
　All, all have lost their spell; and what remains
　Save memory, and troth-plight
　With some far-off delight,
　For Eden's outcast, toiling on hot plains?

WHEN IN THE WOODS I WANDERED.

WHEN in the woods I wandered,
  The gift of bird-like song
  Came on me full and strong;
And many a verse I squandered
  The woods and ways along.

But now my verse, though pondered
  With labor sad and long,
  Strives vainly to be strong.
Ah me! the gift so squandered!
  Ah me! the bird-like song!

THE FORSAKEN DOVE.

ONCE, in the dying day,
    Into the golden skies,
On wings as gold as they
    I watched a wood-dove rise.
Into the shining clouds afar
He shot, and vanished like a star.

But all the moonless night
    I heard in the dark wood
One plaining her sad plight
    In doleful solitude.
O cruel light to take my love!
O lonely night! O forlorn dove!

MAY MEMORIES.

OH, for the light-hearted
　　Life and the passionate
Pulse, and the fetterless
　　　　Feet, and the strong
Stream of enthusiast
Thought, when the spirit of
Spring like a Bacchanal
　　　　Bore me along!
Oh, the luxuriant
Leaves, and the effluent
Flowers, and the resonant
　　　　Raptures of song!

II

Oh, for the mirth-bringing
Morns, and the nectarous
Noons, and the exquisite
   Eves, when the fair
Face of the noiseless queen
Night, with her eloquent
Eyes, and her azure
   Abysses, lay bare;
And like a breath from the
Briar, from the sensitive
Soul rose the innocent
   Incense of prayer!

AFTER STORM.

WIND and wave are sleeping now;
    Leaps no more the lashing surge;
And the lighthouse on the brow
    Glimmers to the distant verge.
Still below, vague and low,
    Croons the sea her solemn dirge.

Sail and seagull all are flown;
    Safe in haven or cleft they lie;
And the stately moon alone
    Moves along the stainless sky.
Still for aye, night and day,
    The sea-voices moan and sigh.

A THOUGHT OF SUMMER.

I WOULD be a cloud
  Half-way up to heaven;
Not aloft and proud,
  Nor too low, and driven
In a whirl of rain
O'er the shivering plain.

But a cloud all white
  In a heaven all blue,
Hanging in men's sight
  Half a long day through,
And when daylight goes,
Dying in soft rose.

OLD AND NEW.

WHERE are they hidden, all the vanished years?
    Ah, who can say!
Where is the laughter flown to, and the tears?
    Perished? Ah, nay!
Beauty and strength are born of sun and showers;
These too shall surely spring again in flowers.

Yet let them sleep, nor seek herein to wed
    Effect to cause,
For Nature's subtlest influences spread
    By viewless laws.
This only seek, that each new year may bring,
Born of past griefs and joys, a fairer spring !

A DEDICATION.

NOT of his treasures gives the sea,
    Not gold or jewels to the land,
Nor of all precious things that he
    Has ravished with his robber hand.
With worthless weeds he wreathes her o'er,
With shells unvalued lines the shore.

Ev'n so his reverent love he shows
    By giving not his costless pelf,
But that which of his being grows,—
    True gift it is to give of self.
For my poor gift let this atone :
I give thee what is most my own.

A DAY OF LOVE.

DEAR is the sunny between-while
  Of April skies,
Though black with storm in the meanwhile
  The clouds arise.

Tho' the clouds that shall burst on the morrow
  Be gathering above,
So dear in a year of sorrow
  Is a day of love.

VIBRATIONS.

WHAT wonder if when Love awakes
    Suddenly the tense heart breaks!
As at the organ's thundering
Breaks the lute's responsive string!

Ah, sadder heart, where Love has grown
Stealthily, his name unknown!
As at some wandering noiseless air
The wind-harp wakens to despair.

AN ENGLISH EDEN.

ROSES drop their petals all around
    In that enchanted ground,
And all the air is murmurous with sound
    From the white-tumbling weir;
So that all sounds or voices heard anear
    Do half unreal appear.

As one half-waking from a dreamless sleep
    Is fain his thought to keep
Thus floating ever 'twixt the night's black deep
    And the blank glare of day:
So in that Eden pauses life midway
    'Twixt dawning and noonday.

AUTUMN SINGERS.

WHEN woods are gold and hedges gay
    With jewelled Autumn's brief array,
And diamonds sprinkle every spray,
    The robin sings
His soft melodious well-a-day
    For dying things.

Yet often, when a riotous night
Has ruined half the wood's delight,
There breaks a spring-day warm and bright;
    And the thrush sings,
As if his April were in sight,
    Of quickening things.

THE END.